Georgia

the Guinea Pig

Fairy

For Tom Powell, with lots of love

Special thanks to Sue Mongredien

No part of this work may be reproduced, stored in a retrieval system, or transmitted in any form or by any means, electronic, mechanical, photocopying, recording, or otherwise, without written permission of the publisher. For information regarding permission, write to Rainbow Magic Limited, c/o HIT Entertainment, 830 South Greenville Avenue, Allen, TX 75002-3320.

ISBN-10: 0-545-04186-4
ISBN-13: 978-0-545-04186-7

17 16 15 14 13 12   13 14/

Printed in the U.S.A.   40

First Scholastic printing, March 2008

Georgia
the Guinea Pig
Fairy

by Daisy Meadows

SCHOLASTIC INC.

New York   Toronto   London   Auckland
Sydney   Mexico City   New Delhi   Hong Kong

The Fairyland Palace

Wetherbury Village

Strawberry Farm

The Spring Show

Jack Frost's Ice Castle

Bramble Stables

Jane Dillon's House

ark

rsty's House

Jamie Cooper's House

The Wainwrights' House

Fairies with their pets I see
and yet no pet has chosen me!
So I will get some of my own
to share my perfect frosty home.

This spell I cast, its aim is clear:
to bring the magic pets straight here.
The Pet Fairies soon will see
their seven pets living with me!

Contents

Farmyard Fun

"This must be one of the cutest animals at Strawberry Farm!" Rachel Walker declared, her eyes shining. She stroked the woolly lamb in her arms. "It's so cuddly!"

"And hungry, too," her best friend, Kirsty Tate, added. She tilted up the bottle of milk she was using to feed the lamb, as a farmhand watched. "It almost finished this already!"

"Just watching it is making me thirsty!" her mom said as the lamb drained the last few drops.

Rachel was staying with Kirsty's family for a week. This afternoon, they were

having a great time at Strawberry Farm!
They had already seen a troop of tiny
ducklings heading out for their first
swim on the pond. They took a pony
ride on a little brown Shetland named
Conker. And now they had the chance
to hand-feed some of the lambs!

Rachel put the lamb down carefully,
and both girls watched it teeter off to join
the other lambs in the field.

"I saw a sign for the Pet Corner over
there," Rachel said, giving Kirsty
a meaningful look. "Should
we go there next?"

Kirsty smiled at her
friend. The two girls
shared a wonderful
secret: They'd been
helping the Pet Fairies all

week! Mean Jack Frost had kidnapped the Pet Fairies' seven magical pets, but the pets had managed to escape into the human world. Yesterday, Rachel and Kirsty had helped Bella the Bunny Fairy find her lost rabbit. And the day before, they'd reunited Katie the Kitten Fairy with her missing kitten. So Kirsty knew exactly what Rachel was hoping: maybe today they'd find another magical pet in the Pet Corner!

"That sounds great, but I think I'll grab a coffee while you two go ahead," Mrs.

Tate said. "I'll meet you both back here at four o'clock."

"Sounds good," Kirsty replied, trying not to seem too enthusiastic. She loved her mom, but she and Rachel always had their very best adventures when they were alone! "See you later."

Mrs. Tate left for the coffee stand, and the two friends headed for the Pet Corner.

"Here we are," Rachel said as they entered an area surrounded by a small fence. "Keep your eyes peeled for magical pets!" she added in an excited whisper.

The girls began looking at all the

rabbits and guinea pigs in the hutches. Every animal had a little sign outside its cage, telling visitors its name and favorite food.

"This rabbit is called Albie, and he likes carrot tops and brussel sprouts," Kirsty read aloud, peeking in at the fluffy gray rabbit. "Hello, Albie!"

"Rosie the guinea pig likes sunflower

seeds and lettuce leaves," Rachel read on another hutch. "Millie, her sister, likes sliced apples. And Carrot, Rosie's baby, likes carrots . . . Oh!"

Kirsty looked up. "What's wrong?" she asked.

Rachel was crouching down and peering into one of the hutches. "There are supposed to be three guinea pigs in

ROSIE, MILLIE & CARROT
Rosie likes sunflower seeds and lettuce leaves. Millie, her sister likes sliced apples, and Carrot, Rosie's baby, likes carrots and banana skins.

here — Millie, Rosie, and baby Carrot," she told Kirsty. "But the baby guinea pig is missing!"

Kirsty hurried over.

"Oh no, look," she said. "The cage door is open — Carrot must have escaped!"

Out of the corner of her eye, Rachel spotted a flash of fur behind the hutches. She turned to see a small orange-and-white guinea pig squeezing under the

ROSIE, MILLIE & CARROT
Rosie likes sunflower seeds and lettuce leaves. Millie, her sister, likes sliced apple, and Carrot, Rosie's baby, likes carrots and banana sk

wooden fence. "That must be Carrot over there!" she cried.

Kirsty shut the cage door firmly, then jumped up to look. "Oh, no — he's heading for the field of sheep!" she said, pointing.

Rachel ran off after the little guinea pig, looking worried. "He's too young to be out on his own," she said. "We have to rescue him, Kirsty!"

Magic in Midair!

Kirsty and Rachel climbed over the wooden fence surrounding the field of sheep, and hurried after the guinea pig. Carrot was scampering toward a tree on the far side of the field. When the guinea pig reached the base of the tree, both girls stopped and stared in disbelief. Instead of swerving around the tree, the little animal simply ran straight up the trunk!

"I didn't think guinea pigs could do that!" Kirsty gasped. "I'll go after him, in case he gets stuck."

Kirsty clambered up the tree, picking her way from branch to branch until she was within arm's reach of the little guinea pig. Carrot watched her curiously. "Hello," Kirsty said in a soft voice, reaching out toward him. As she did, the guinea pig twitched its nose and backed away playfully.

Kirsty stretched out her hand a little further. "Come here, little Carrot," she said. Again the guinea pig backed away, and Kirsty thought she glimpsed a mischievous little smile on its face!

"I'm imagining things now," Kirsty said to herself. She inched further along the branch and then leaned out, trying to reach the guinea pig. Just as her fingertips were about to touch Carrot's fur, he jumped right off the branch . . . and scampered away through the air!

Kirsty nearly fell out of the tree in surprise. "Rachel, look!" she cried excitedly, scrambling back down to the ground.

Rachel felt a thrill as she realized what was happening. "That's not Carrot, the farm guinea pig," she laughed. "It's Georgia the Guinea Pig Fairy's magic pet!" She and Kirsty had met all of the Pet Fairies in Fairyland. "I wonder where Georgia is."

At that very moment, the girls heard the sound of cheerful singing above them. They looked up to see Georgia swooping toward them on the back of a blackbird!

"Georgia!" Rachel cried, waving at the pretty fairy.

Georgia waved back cheerfully as the blackbird perched above the girls on a tree branch. She had short black hair and wore a yellow top and suede skirt, both fringed with turquoise beads and tassels. She smiled as she slipped off the blackbird's back and thanked it for the ride. The blackbird sung a merry reply and fluttered away.

Georgia flew over to Rachel's shoulder.

Her gauzy wings shimmered in the sunlight. "Hello, girls," she said, in a bright, friendly voice.

"We were looking for a lost guinea pig named Carrot," Kirsty explained eagerly. "But we found your magic pet instead, Georgia!"

Georgia twirled excitedly when she heard the good news. "I thought he was somewhere near here!" she declared, looking around. "Oh, Sparky, hello!" she called, seeing  the little orange-and-white guinea pig trotting along in midair. "I've missed you so much!" Rachel smiled as Sparky squeaked happily to his fairy owner and began scampering toward her.

Georgia listened to Sparky's eager squeaks. "He says that he's been looking for Carrot, too," she told the girls. "And —"

But before Georgia could translate any more of Sparky's message, one of the sheep that had been grazing nearby suddenly stood up on its hind legs. To everybody's amazement, the sheep had a butterfly net. It swept the net through the air and captured Sparky!

"Hey!" Kirsty cried. "What's going on?"

"That's not a sheep," Rachel called
out in horror. A long green nose
poked out from the creature's face. "It's a
goblin in disguise!"

Goblins Undercover

A gleeful cackle rang through the air. The goblin ran across the field with Sparky trapped in the butterfly net.

"Oh, no!" Kirsty cried. "What are we going to do now?"

"I'll turn you into fairies so we can all fly after him," Georgia said quickly,

waving her wand over the girls. A stream
of glittering turquoise sparkles swirled
from the tip of her wand and whirled
around Kirsty and Rachel. In an
instant, both girls shrank down into
tiny fairies.

Rachel fluttered her
shimmering wings,
feeling light as she
floated off the ground.
Being a fairy was the
best thing in the whole

world! But now, the
girls had work to do.
"Let's follow that
sneaky goblin!" Rachel
cried, zooming through
the air after him.

"Don't worry, Sparky, we're coming!" Kirsty called out, following Rachel.

But as they flew over the field, several more sheep jumped up on their back legs and began swiping at Kirsty, Rachel, and Georgia with butterfly nets. There were more goblins in sheep disguises!

"Now they're chasing us!" Rachel warned, looking over her shoulder. The

goblins raced after them with nets in their hands and nasty grins on their faces.

"Fly higher," Georgia urged the girls. "Don't let them catch you, too!"

Kirsty, Rachel, and Georgia flew out of reach of the goblins. The goblin who had caught Sparky ran into a big, old barn and the girls zipped in after him.

It was very dark inside, and at first the three friends

couldn't see very much in the gloom.
But then Georgia muttered a
few magical words. The
turquoise tip of her wand
glowed brightly, like a
glittering blue torch.
"Sparky, where
are you?" she
called softly,
fluttering over to
look behind a
stack of hay bales.
Kirsty and Rachel
were also flying
around the barn,
hoping to catch a
glimpse of the guinea pig.
Suddenly, Sparky
gave a couple of high-pitched

squeaks. Kirsty, Rachel, and Georgia
flew toward the sound at once.

The magic pet's squeaks seemed to
be coming from somewhere near the
barn door.

Unfortunately, just as the girls and
Georgia approached the door, the other
goblins ran into the barn. They cackled
with delight to see the three fairies

caught off-guard and hovering in front of them.

"Catch them!" one of the goblins yelled, swinging his net around in an attempt to capture the fairies.

"Oh, no, you don't!" Georgia cried. She and the girls soared upward, away from the goblins.

Kirsty managed to dodge one goblin who made a grab for her, but the tallest one had her in his sights.

Kirsty flew up just as the goblin swished his butterfly net down — she was trapped!

"Help!" she cried, beating her wings frantically.

"Ha!" the tall goblin smirked, putting a warty green hand over the top of the net. "You're my prisoner now!"

Trapped!

Georgia grabbed Rachel's hand. She pulled her up to a small, broken window above the barn door just as the goblins swung the door shut with a thump.

"What are we going to do?" Rachel asked Georgia. Her heart was beating wildly as they squeezed through the hole in the window. "The goblins are holding Kirsty prisoner!"

Georgia's eyes narrowed. "Don't worry, we'll free her," she vowed. "We just need to

think of a way to rescue Kirsty and Sparky — fast!"

Rachel and Georgia fell silent as they thought about what to do. They could hear the goblins hooting triumphantly inside the barn.

"A guinea pig *and* a fairy," one of them crowed. "What a day!"

"Jack Frost is going to be happy with us today," another added smugly.

Then Rachel and Georgia heard a scraping noise as the goblins slid the bolt across the barn door, locking it.

"We'll sit tight until those two fairies have gone," one goblin muttered. "Then we'll take this fairy and the guinea pig back to Jack Frost's castle."

Rachel thought it was horrible to hear the goblins gloating. She perched on the window frame, thinking hard. "Georgia, do you think Sparky might be able to turn himself into an elephant and knock the door down?" she asked.

Georgia shook her head sadly. "Sparky won't be able to use

any magic," she told Rachel. "None of the magic pets can use magic when they're afraid." She frowned, concentrating. "We'll have to make the goblins leave the barn somehow," she went on. "Maybe we could tempt them out with something to eat?"

Rachel grinned as an idea suddenly popped into her head. "Or we could *scare* them out," she said eagerly. "Georgia, do you think you could use magic to create the sound of an angry bull?"

"Of course," Georgia replied. Then she grinned as she realized what Rachel had in mind. "Of course! The sound of an angry bull that has been woken by noisy goblins will be just the thing to drive them from the barn!" she whispered with a chuckle.

Rachel nodded happily. "The goblins will never know that it's only fairy magic they are hearing," she added.

Georgia and Rachel grinned at each other, then fluttered down to the ground.

"Let's give it a try," Georgia said. "The sooner we free Kirsty and Sparky, the sooner we can find little Carrot."

She waved her wand, sending more turquoise sparkles swirling around Rachel.

In an instant, Rachel grew back to her usual size.

Then Georgia pointed her wand at the  barn doors. They shimmered for a few seconds with magical turquoise light. "There," she whispered to Rachel. "I've used magic to hold the doors shut. Even if the goblins unbolt them, they won't be able to come out until we let them."

Rachel smiled. "And we'll only let them out when they promise to hand over Kirsty and Sparky," she whispered back. "It's a great idea, Georgia!" Then, with a wink at the smiling fairy, Rachel

raised her voice. "Beware of the bull?"
she said, as if she were reading aloud
from a sign. "I wonder if those goblins
know they're stuck in the barn with
Farmer Tom's mean old bull? It's got a
bad temper — it's way too crazy to be
out in the fields." She laughed loudly. "I
wouldn't want to be in there when the
bull wakes up!"

Rachel glanced up at Georgia, who was hovering outside the window above the barn door. With a wave of her wand, the little fairy sent a stream of magic all the way into the darkest corner of the barn.

Snort! Grunt! CRASH! A terrible commotion started where Georgia's magic had landed. There was a thunderous, hoof-stamping sound.

Georgia flew back down to perch on Rachel's shoulder. She tried not to laugh out loud at their clever trick.

Rachel pressed her ear to the barn door to listen to the goblins.

"Whose stupid idea was it to come in here, anyway?" one of them hissed nervously.

"Farmer Tom's crazy b-b-bull sounds really a-a-angry!" another goblin stuttered.

Rachel and Georgia heard the sound of the bolt being pulled back. Then one

of the goblins tried to push the door
open, but Georgia's magic held the door
firmly shut.

"You're trapped in there," Rachel
called, "with Farmer Tom's crazy bull!"

"Maybe the bull will make a nice pet
for Jack Frost," Georgia suggested
sweetly.

"Hey, let us out right now!" a goblin
demanded, thumping on
the door.

"I don't think
so," Georgia
replied in her
silvery fairy
voice. Then
she zoomed up
to the window and

waved her wand again, sending more magic into the barn. Immediately, the roar of an angry bull started up again, but this time it sounded even louder! "Oh, all that shouting seems to have made the bull even angrier!" Georgia remarked.

The goblins hammered on the door in panic. "Let us out right now!" they cried.

Girls and Goblins Agree

"You let Kirsty and Sparky go, and then we'll let you out of the barn!" Rachel shouted to the goblins.

There was a minute of silence. "We can't tell Jack Frost that we've let another of those pesky pets slip through our fingers," Rachel heard one goblin whisper.

"First we messed up the kitten kidnap, then the bunny bagging. If we come back today without the guinea pig —"

"We *can't* go back without the guinea pig," another goblin interrupted. "But how about if we . . ."

Rachel pressed her ear as close to the barn door as possible, but the goblins were talking so quietly now that she couldn't hear what they were plotting.

"The fairy can go, but the guinea pig's staying with us!" a goblin voice announced after a moment.

Rachel looked at Georgia sadly. She hadn't been expecting that response! "What do we say?" she whispered.

"Let's agree, and then at least we'll know that Kirsty's safe," Georgia replied. "Maybe one of you will be able to grab Sparky as the goblins come out of the barn."

Rachel nodded. "OK," she said reluctantly. Then she turned back to the barn door.

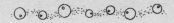

"It's a deal," she shouted to the goblins.
"Set Kirsty free!"

A moment passed while Rachel and
Georgia waited to see if the goblins were
plotting a trick of their own. Then Kirsty
zoomed out of the window and flew
down to join them, smiling with relief.

Georgia waved her wand and turned
Kirsty back into a girl.

Rachel hugged her tightly. "Are you all right? Were they mean to you and Sparky?" she asked.

"I'm fine," Kirsty said. "And so is Sparky. He's being very quiet, but he isn't hurt."

A loud knocking came from the other side of the barn door. "A deal's a deal," one of the goblins yelled. "Open up before this crazy bull finds us!"

Georgia pointed her wand at the doors.

"We're going to try and grab the goblin who has Sparky, OK?" Rachel whispered to Kirsty.

Kirsty nodded. "He was standing behind the others, at the back," she told Rachel quietly. "Ready when you are, Georgia."

Georgia waved her wand. The barn doors glittered with bright blue light again, then burst open. The goblins immediately raced out of the barn.

"Quick! Before the bull starts chasing us!" one of them shrieked.

Kirsty and Rachel lunged for the last goblin, who was clutching Sparky. Their hands closed around empty air as he nimbly dodged them and sprinted away across the field.

"He's getting away!" cried Rachel.

Kirsty looked around frantically for something she could use to stop the goblin. Suddenly, she

spotted some old rope just inside the barn. "Georgia, could you use your magic to turn that rope into a lasso for me?" she asked quickly.

"Yes," the fairy replied, waving her wand. Turquoise fairy dust spiralled through the air. The frayed old rope turned into a lasso and flew straight up into Kirsty's hand. Kirsty swung the loop of the lasso around her head, keeping

her eyes fixed on the goblin who was
running off with Sparky. Then she
launched the lasso straight at him.

The girls held their breath as the lasso

sailed through the air. It seemed to be heading in the wrong direction, but Georgia quickly pointed her wand at it. The lasso shone with blue magic and veered back on course, toward the goblin. The loop of rope fell right over his head and caught tight around his middle, pinning his arms by his sides.

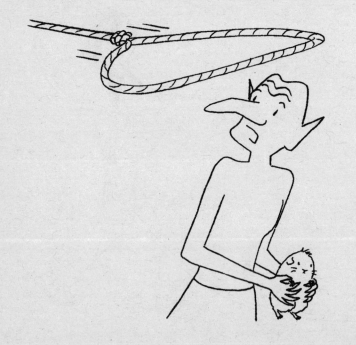

The goblin tried to keep running, but the rope pulled itself magically out of Kirsty's hands and wound itself around the goblin's legs until he had to stop.

"Got him!" Kirsty cheered triumphantly.

Odd One Out

"Help!" the lassoed goblin yelled to his friends, but they were too busy running away from the imaginary bull to notice.

Rachel and Kirsty walked calmly over to the struggling goblin. Sparky, who was still in the goblin's hands, squeaked hello.

"Come here, Sparky," Rachel said, gently lifting him out of the goblin's hands.

Sparky squeaked even louder when he saw Georgia fluttering in midair. With a twitch of his nose, he jumped up toward her. As he leaped through the air, he shrank to his usual tiny size. Georgia picked him up happily and gave him a big hug.

"Hey! What about me?" the goblin shouted angrily, still tangled in the rope.

Georgia smiled at him. "Don't worry, the magic will wear off the rope soon," she assured him. "In a couple of hours or so, you'll be free . . ."

"A couple of hours?" the goblin groaned.

Georgia winked at Kirsty and Rachel as they walked back toward the Pet Corner. "It will only be a couple of minutes, really," she whispered with a laugh.

Sparky started squeaking urgently, and suddenly Georgia looked worried. "Of course!" she cried. "We have to find poor little Carrot! I'd almost forgotten about him."

Rachel looked at her watch. "It's a quarter to four already," she said. "Kirsty, we have to meet your mom in fifteen minutes. We don't have much time to look for Carrot."

"Then I'll turn you back into fairies,"
Georgia said, waving her wand briskly.
"That way, we can all fly around and
look for him. Let's split up and meet back
at Carrot's hutch in five minutes."

Rachel and Kirsty
zoomed off in different
directions, searching
for the lost, little
guinea pig. Kirsty
checked out the play
area, the cow barn, and
even popped through the windows of the
gift shop. Rachel hunted
around the pig pen, the
duck pond, and the
stables. There was no
sign of Carrot
anywhere.

"I don't understand it," Georgia said when they met up with her again five minutes later. "Where could he be?"

"We should go soon," Rachel said sadly, "but I can't leave the farm without knowing that Carrot's safe!"

Kirsty suddenly pointed ahead to where a mother hen was being followed by a line of her chicks. "Wait a minute," she said, narrowing her eyes. "That's a strange-looking chick at the end of the line!"

Rachel looked where Kirsty was pointing, and then giggled in relief. The

last "chick" in the line was not yellow
and fluffy, like the others. It was a small,
carrot-colored guinea pig!

"Carrot's adopted a new family!"
Georgia chuckled. "How sweet!"

Sparky scampered over to Carrot and
squeaked at him happily. Georgia,
Rachel, and Kirsty watched as Carrot

looked at Sparky, then back at the
chicks, as if he was figuring something
out. Then he rubbed noses with Sparky
and squeaked.

Georgia grinned. "He says he's enjoyed
being part of the hen family, but he's
ready to go home now," she translated.
"And we're ready, too, little Carrot!"

Georgia checked to make sure that
nobody else was in sight. Then she
waved her wand over Rachel and Kirsty,

turning them back into girls. Kirsty went over and picked up Carrot. "Come on," she said gently. "Let's take you back to your hutch."

As soon as Kirsty had placed Carrot back in his hutch, Rosie and Millie, Carrot's mom and aunt, rushed over and squeaked at Carrot excitedly. Then all three of them rubbed noses, and Carrot nestled against Rosie, looking very happy.

Georgia waved her wand to make sure that the cage door was tightly shut. "There will be

no more going back to the hen
house, OK?" she said to Carrot, with
a smile.

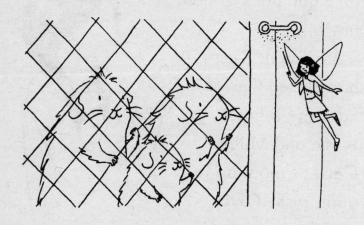

Then she picked up Sparky and turned
to the girls. "It's almost four o'clock.
You'd better go," she told them. "And
we should fly back to Fairyland,
Sparky — where I'm going to make sure
that Jack Frost never gets anywhere near
you again!"

Sparky nuzzled Georgia's arm and she pet him gently. "Thank you for everything," she said to Kirsty and Rachel. "Sparky says thank you, too."

Kirsty and Rachel hugged the tiny fairy good-bye and gave Sparky a gentle scratch. Sparky squeaked good-bye to the girls, then squeaked in the direction of Carrot's cage. A bunch of squeaks came back in reply, as if the farm guinea pigs were calling out their good-byes, too.

And then, with a burst of turquoise sparkles that glittered in the afternoon sunlight, Georgia and Sparky vanished.

"There you are, girls!" came a voice. Rachel and Kirsty turned to see Mrs. Tate walking toward them. "Have you had a nice day?"

"Great, thanks, Mom," Kirsty replied with a smile. "Wasn't it, Rachel?"

"Oh, yes," Rachel agreed. She grinned as she noticed a pot of sunflower seeds, some sliced apple, and a whole

pile of carrot sticks in the guinea pigs'
cage. She was sure
that the food was a
gift from Georgia!
It definitely hadn't
been there before.
"Today's been
magical!" Rachel said,
sighing happily.

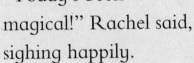

Georgia the Guinea Pig Fairy
has her pet back.
Now Rachel and Kirsty must help

Lauren
the Puppy
Fairy!

Puppies on Show

"Look at that zucchini, Kirsty!" Rachel
Walker laughed, pointing at the giant
green vegetable on the display table. "It's
almost as big as I am!"

Kirsty Tate read the card propped
in front of the zucchini. "It won a
prize," she announced. "It's the

biggest vegetable at the Wetherbury Spring Show!"

There were other enormous vegetables on the table, too. The girls stared at the giant-size carrots and onions. There were also huge bowls of daffodils, tulips, and bluebells. The best flower displays had won prizes, too.

"This is great!" Rachel declared. "I wish we had a Spring Show back home."

Rachel was staying in Wetherbury with Kirsty for the week, and the girls had spent the whole afternoon at the show. The field was crammed with booths selling homemade cakes, cookies, and jams, and there were pony rides and a huge red-and-yellow bouncy castle. Rachel and Kirsty were having a great time!

"I think we've been around the whole show," Kirsty said at last. "Mom and Dad will be here to pick us up soon."

"Should we take one last look at our favorite booth?" Rachel asked eagerly.

"You mean the one for the Wetherbury Animal Shelter?" Kirsty said with a smile.

Rachel nodded. "I want to see if they've found homes for those four puppies."

"I hope so," Kirsty said. "They were really cute! And speaking of pets . . ." She lowered her voice so that she wouldn't be overheard. "Do you think we might find another fairy pet today?"

"We'll just have to keep our eyes open!" Rachel whispered in a determined voice.

RAINBOW magic™

There's Magic in Every Series!

The Rainbow Fairies

The Weather Fairies

The Jewel Fairies

The Pet Fairies

The Fun Day Fairies

The Petal Fairies

The Dance Fairies

Read them all!

SCHOLASTIC

www.scholastic.com
www.rainbowmagiconline.com

HiT entertainment

RMFAI

RAINBOW magic™

SPECIAL EDITION

More Rainbow Magic Fun!
Three Stories in One!

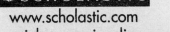

These activities are magical!